12-11

SpongeBob SquarePants

CHRISTMAS KRABBY KLAWS

by Erica David

illustrated by Heather Martinez

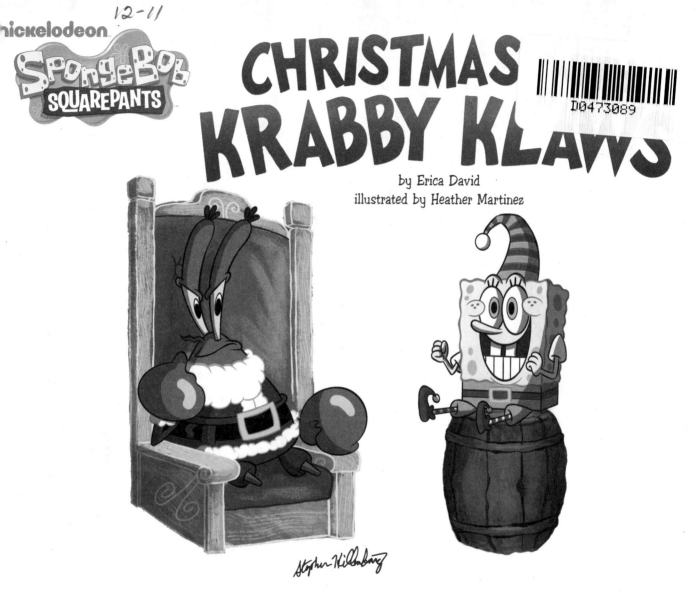

Stephen Hillenburg

Based on the TV series *SpongeBob SquarePants*™ created by Stephen Hillenburg as seen on Nickelodeon™

SIMON SPOTLIGHT/NICKELODEON
An imprint of Simon & Schuster Children's Publishing Division
New York   London   Toronto   Sydney
1230 Avenue of the Americas, New York, New York 10020

For information about special discounts for bulk purchases, please contact Simon & Schuster Special Sales at 1·866·506·1949 or business@simonandschuster.com.
Manufactured in the United States of America   0910 COM   First Edition   2 4 6 8 10 9 7 5 3 1
ISBN 978-1-4424-0805-0

The holidays were in full swing in Bikini Bottom. Even Mr. Krabs was filled with Christmas spirit. He had turned the Krusty Krab into a winter wonderland. SpongeBob was the head elf in charge of holiday cheer.

"Step right up, boys and girls," SpongeBob said. "Ride the reindeer seahorse carousel, join the candy-cane scavenger hunt, or have your picture taken with Krabby Klaws!"

"Ho, ho, ho! That's right, mateys. The fun is free, but the activities will cost you a small fee, of course," added Mr. Krabs.

"We love you, Krabby Klaws!" the children shouted with delight.

Mr. Krabs opened the cash register. It was full of money—just the way he liked it.

"SpongeBob, me boy, these holiday activities were a great idea!" he said, giving SpongeBob a hearty pat on the back.

"The kids really seem to like it," SpongeBob agreed.

"Like it? They love it—especially Krabby Klaws!" Mr. Krabs exclaimed. "I bet he's more popular now than Santa himself!"

SpongeBob gasped. "Take that back, Mr. Krabs! You don't want Santa to be angry with you, do you?"

"Angry? Who could be angry with Krabby Klaws?" asked Mr. Krabs, laughing his jolly laugh.

SpongeBob was worried. He knew that Santa Claus heard and saw everything. How else would he know who's been naughty or nice?

Just then a large sleigh decoration fell to the ground with a *CRASH*! It almost landed right on top of Mr. Krabs! SpongeBob was scared.

"It's a sign from Santa, Mr. Krabs!" SpongeBob cried.

"Oh, don't be silly, lad!" Mr. Krabs replied with a shrug.

SpongeBob had a bad feeling about the sleigh,
but he tried not to think about it.
"Gather around, kids. It's time to have your
pictures taken with Krabby Klaws," he announced.

SpongeBob pulled out the camera, and the children lined up to sit on Krabby Klaws's lap. But as soon as SpongeBob snapped a photo, the camera exploded in a puff of smoke.

"Oh, no!" SpongeBob said. "First the sleigh, now the camera! These are bad signs!"

"Signs, shmigns," said Mr. Krabs, ignoring SpongeBob's fears.

With the camera broken, Mr. Krabs encouraged everyone to buy Krabby Patties instead.

In the kitchen SpongeBob was busy tossing patties on the grill. All of a sudden the grill made a weird noise. It creaked and groaned, and smoke began to pour out from the sides.

"Holy Krabby Patties!" cried SpongeBob.

Mr. Krabs poked his head into the kitchen. "What's going on here?"

"The grill is broken!" SpongeBob said. "Don't you see? It's Santa! He's angry, Mr. Krabs. You have to apologize and make things right! Please!"

That night was Christmas Eve. SpongeBob made Mr. Krabs stay up late to wait for Santa and apologize. They fixed the grill and cooked a special plate of Krabby Patties just for him. They waited and waited, but still there was no sign of Santa. At last they fell asleep.

When they woke up the next morning, the Krabby Patties were gone. In their place was a note from Santa. Mr. Krabs read the note aloud:

"Dear Krabby Klaws, I was happy when you decided to bring holiday cheer to the children of Bikini Bottom, but sad to discover that your selfish, money-hungry ways caused you to lose sight of what is important. If you don't learn the meaning of being selfless, I will be forced to put you on the naughty list. Try giving a gift without expecting something in return. I know in the end you'll do the right thing. Love, Santa Claus."

"Don't worry, Mr. Krabs!" said SpongeBob. "I've got a plan. No friend of mine is going on the naughty list!"

It was Christmas Day, and the Krusty Krab was filled with people. "Step right up, boys and girls," SpongeBob said. "Ride the reindeer seahorse carousel, join the candy-cane scavenger hunt, or have your picture taken with Krabby Klaws!"

"Ho, ho, ho. That's right, mateys. It's Christmas, and today all food and activities are . . . free," Mr. Krabs grumbled under his breath.

"I didn't hear you, Krabby Klaws," SpongeBob said.

"*FREE!*" Mr. Krabs shouted.

"That's the spirit, Krabby Klaws!" SpongeBob replied. "Santa is going to be so proud of you!"

That night after the Krusty Krab closed, SpongeBob gathered everyone around the tree to open their presents.

When it was Mr. Krabs's turn, he picked up a golden sack with an unfamiliar card. It was from Santa. He read the card aloud.

"Dear Krabby Klaws, I see you've learned that Christmas is about giving, not getting. You've done me proud! Please accept this as a reminder of the spirit of the holiday. Merry Christmas!"

Mr. Krabs opened the present. It was a framed page from Santa's nice list with Mr. Krabs's name on it: Eugene.

"It feels pretty good to be on the nice list," Mr. Krabs confessed. "Krabby Klaws did make a lot of kids happy today."

"See, Mr. Krabs?" SpongeBob said. "Being nice is truly the greatest gift of all!"

"Hey, how did Santa know that Mr. Krabs would do the right thing?" Patrick asked the gang.

"Of course he knew, Patrick," SpongeBob cried out, happily. "He's Santa Claus!"